Brave

Heather Leughmyer

Illustrated by April Pedersen

WHO Chains YOU PUBLISHING .com

Published by Who Chains You Books
P.O. Box 581
Amissville, VA 20106
WhoChainsYou.com

Written by Heather Leughmyer
Illustrated by April Pedersen

ISBN-10: 1-946044-14-8
ISBN-13: 978-1-946044-14-3

Printed in the United States of America

First Edition

This book is dedicated to
our wild bat friends and the rehabbers
who care for them

Benny the bat always did what was right; hiding during the day and hunting at night. Benny loved bugs, so scrumptious and sweet; moths were mouth-watering, and mosquitos a treat!

His bed was a tree and he slept upside down, in a quaint little forest just outside of town. Each night at dusk he'd stretch and he'd yawn, then drop out of bed, and be home before dawn.

All of the bats would flap, fly, and dive, filling stomachs with bugs until daylight arrived.

By daybreak the bats would be sleeping away, but bored little Benny still wanted to play.

He was ready to feel the sun on his face; to flap, fly, and dive in a whole different place.

He wished to discover the world in the light; he was tired of darkness, fed up with the night. Then one dewy morning, he passed by his tree; he was nervous, but eager, about what he would see.

He flew out of the forest, past a field and a farm. "It's peaceful," thought Benny. "No cause for alarm."

His mother had warned him, "There is danger" she said. "You must only come out when the world is in bed."

ut Benny was smart, daring and brave; he wanted more out of life than just a tree or a cave. At first Benny's eyes weren't used to the light, but his echolocation was as useful as sight.

When he finally opened his tiny black eyes, little Benny was in for a giant surprise. For Benny then realized he wasn't alone, and its shadow had MUCH bigger wings than his own!

A huge brown hawk swooped down from on high. "Mmm," said the bird, "a snack in the sky!"

"Wait!" Benny shrieked. He was now full of fear. "I'm MUCH less delicious than I may appear!"

The hawk suddenly seemed far less than amused. "Why aren't you sleeping?" he asked, "I'm confused."

"I'm exploring," chirped Benny, in a small, shaky voice.

"I have to eat," said the bird. "I don't have a choice."

"Try bugs!" Benny cried, "You would really like those!"

The hawk let out a laugh, "I'll let you go, I suppose."

Benny was grateful, and he felt very lucky. Then he thought to himself, "A bat *would* taste yucky."

Benny continued his journey, his dreams were immense. Adventure was calling, just over that fence.

When the town was in sight, Benny felt slightly stressed; he wondered if he'd be an unwelcome guest. He took a deep breath, as he passed the first street. He flew over a house and his heart skipped a beat.

"This might not go well," he thought with a sigh; but he didn't turn back, he continued to fly.

He'd heard of the creatures that lived in this town; they didn't have wings or sleep upside down! His mother had told him to stay far away, from these baffling beings that came out in the day.

But Benny was stubborn, and he liked to explore; it was then that he spotted a wide open door. He flapped and he flew until he was inside, then he quickly observed, there was nowhere to hide.

It was nothing like home—where were the trees? Where were the insects, like beetles and bees?

He dodged around creatures, both big and small; he had nowhere to go, without hitting a wall.

He was frightened and homesick, and done with the day, but he didn't quite know just how he'd get away.

He heard someone scream, "That's no bird, it's a bat!" And before Benny knew it, he was under a hat.

Benny quivered and shivered; he wanted his tree. If he had listened to mother, right now he'd be free. The creatures were speaking; such odd sounds they were making. Benny waited and worried, his whole body shaking.

Trapped in a hat, Benny wanted to cry, then surprisingly it opened up to the sun and the sky!

Benny flapped fragile wings and flew very fast, refusing to rest 'til he was home at last. He had some time to sleep, before the stars shined bright.

He decided then and there, that he preferred the night.

The End

Some Batty Questions

1. Do you know what echolocation is?

2. Why are bats important to the eco-system?

3. What would you do if a bat got into your house?

Good Batty Answers

1. Echolocation, also called bio sonar, is the biological sonar used by several kinds of animals, including bats like Benny. The animals emit calls out to the environment and then listen to the echoes of those calls as they bounce off and return to them from various objects nearby. They then use these echoes to locate and identify the objects. Echolocation is used for navigation and for foraging or hunting in various environments.

2. Bats consume many insects, such as mosquitoes, that we consider pests. Some bats catch and consume up to 2,000 insects per night. Bats also help keep crops, flowers, and fruits free of pests; they also help pollinate many plants and disperse seeds so that new plants can grow. Many species of bats are endangered, and some are on the verge of extinction. It is important that we protect bats and remember that they are vital to the survival of ecosystems around the world.

3. If you have a bat flying around inside your house, don't panic! They are not going to attack you. They really just want to get outside because they feel trapped. **Here are some humane options for relocating a bat back outside:**

Never try to do this yourself! Always get an adult to catch the bat. Bats are not aggressive but they will try to defend themselves if they feel threatened, and you do not want to get bitten.

OPTION 1: Open all the doors (and windows if there are no screens.) Bats have good echolocation and they may realize the window or door is open and then simply fly out.

OPTION 2: If you turn on all the lights a bat will usually roost somewhere which makes them easier to catch. You can use a butterfly net, but be careful when closing the top not to crush the fragile bat. You can also use a bowl, a bucket, or even a hat. Wait for the bat to land and then carefully place the item over the bat against a wall, ceiling, or floor. Slide a piece of paper between the wall and item you are using to contain the bat, and then take them outside and let them go.

OPTION 3: Drape a blanket or towel over the bat, then gently bunch it up, take the bat outside, and let them go.

No matter what method you are using, remember to always be gentle. Bats have very delicate bones in their wings, so be very careful not to injure them!

Activities for Kids

COLOR ME !

START

About the Author

Heather Leughmyer graduated from Indiana-Purdue University with a B.A. in English Writing and Linguistics. She is a dedicated vegan, animal rights activist, and animal rescuer. Writing has been a passion of hers for as long as she has advocated for animals.

Heather lives in Columbia City, Indiana, with her husband, daughter and several animal companions. She is also the author of ***Adopting Adele, If Your Tears Were Human, A Rat's Guide to Owning a Human,*** and co-editor of ***Rescue Smiles.***

About the Illustrator

Our whimsical artist, **April Pedersen,** is a freelancer based in Reno, Nevada. She is partial to frogs, geocaching, science fiction, video poker, and chess. April is also the illustrator of ***Adopting Adele.***

PLEASE REMEMBER TO RESPECT AND PROTECT OUR BATS

Love this book? We hope you'll give *Brave Benny* a review on Amazon and other venues. Your reviews mean so much to our authors. Thank you!